獻給喜愛蝸牛的海斯特
—— C.R. 與 A.S.

♥ IREAD

皮皮與波西：小蝸牛

文　　　字	卡蜜拉·里德
繪　　　圖	阿克賽爾·薛弗勒
譯　　　者	酪梨壽司
責任編輯	江奕萱
美術編輯	郭雅萍

發 行 人	劉振強
出 版 者	三民書局股份有限公司
地　　　址	臺北市復興北路 386 號 (復北門市) 臺北市重慶南路一段 61 號 (重南門市)
電　　　話	(02)25006600
網　　　址	三民網路書店 https://www.sanmin.com.tw

出版日期	初版一刷 2021 年 8 月 初版二刷 2022 年 6 月
書籍編號	S859460
I S B N	978-957-14-7247-8

Text Copyright © Camilla Reid 2020
Illustrations Copyright © Axel Scheffler 2020
This translation of Pip and Posy: The Friendly Snail is published by
arrangement with Nosy Crow ® Limited
Traditional Chinese translation rights © 2021 San Min Book Co., Ltd.

小山丘官網

皮皮與波西

皮皮與波西
小蝸牛

卡蜜拉·里德╱文　阿克賽爾·薛弗勒╱圖　酪梨壽司╱譯

小山丘

今天天氣真好。
皮皮在院子裡種東西。

波西在玩耍。

「咚！咚！」她打著鼓。
「啦！啦！」她唱著歌。

「砰（ㄆㄥ）！砰（ㄆㄥ）！」她（ㄊㄚ）跳（ㄊㄠˋ）來（ㄌㄞˊ）跳（ㄊㄠˋ）去（ㄑㄩˋ）。

「波（ㄅㄛ）西（ㄒㄧ），可（ㄎㄜˇ）以（ㄧˇ）請（ㄑㄧㄥˇ）妳（ㄋㄧˇ）小（ㄒㄧㄠˇ）聲（ㄕㄥ）一（ㄧ）點（ㄉㄧㄢˇ）嗎（ㄇㄚ）？」皮（ㄆㄧˊ）皮（ㄆㄧˊ）說（ㄕㄨㄛ）。

就在這時候，皮皮發現一隻蝸牛。
一隻非常友善的蝸牛。

「耶！」波西說。

「噓，波西。」皮皮說。

皮皮餵蝸牛吃一些萵苣葉。
蝸牛看起來很開心。

波西來了。

「轟！轟！轟！」她大喊。

蝸牛縮回牠的殼裡。

「波西！」皮皮說。
「妳嚇到我的蝸牛了！
妳玩的遊戲太吵了！走開！」

波西很難過。
她不是故意要嚇蝸牛的。

可憐的波西！

皮ㄆㄧˊ皮ㄆㄧˊ翻ㄈㄢ鬆ㄙㄨㄥ泥ㄋㄧˊ土ㄊㄨˇ。

他ㄊㄚ種ㄓㄨㄥˋ下ㄒㄧㄚˋ一一些ㄒㄧㄝ種ㄓㄨㄥˇ子ㄗˇ。

接著他用灑水壺為種子澆水。

皮皮沒注意到有隻鳥正盯著蝸牛看。

鳥兒逼近蝸牛。越來越近。

越來越近！

喔，天啊！

「吼ㄏㄡˋ喔ㄛ喔ㄛ喔ㄛ喔ㄛ！」有ㄧㄡˇ個ㄍㄜ聲ㄕㄥ音ㄧㄣ大ㄉㄚˋ吼ㄏㄡˋ。
皮ㄆㄧˊ皮ㄆㄧˊ嚇ㄒㄧㄚˋ得ㄉㄜ跳ㄊㄧㄠˋ起ㄑㄧˇ來ㄌㄞˊ。

「走ㄗㄡˇ開ㄎㄞ，你ㄋㄧˇ這ㄓㄜˋ隻ㄓ貪ㄊㄢ吃ㄔ的ㄉㄜ大ㄉㄚˋ鳥ㄋㄧㄠˇ！」
那ㄋㄚˋ個ㄍㄜˋ聲ㄕㄥ音ㄧㄣ又ㄧㄡˋ大ㄉㄚˋ喊ㄏㄢˇ。

鳥ㄋㄧㄠˇ兒ㄦˊ飛ㄈㄟ上ㄕㄤ天ㄊㄧㄢ……

而ㄦˊ蝸ㄍㄨㄚ牛ㄋㄧㄡˊ掉ㄉㄧㄠˋ在ㄗㄞˋ地ㄉㄧˋ上ㄕㄤˋ。

波西從樹叢後面走出來。

「喔，波西，」皮皮說。
「原來是妳！
妳的大叫聲救了蝸牛！」

「對不起，波西，」皮皮說。
「有時候吵鬧也是件好事。

我ㄨㄛˇ們ㄇㄣ˙可ㄎㄜˇ以ㄧˇ和ㄏㄜˊ好ㄏㄠˇ嗎ㄇㄚ˙？」

「好ㄏㄠˇ啊ㄚ˙，當ㄉㄤ然ㄖㄢˊ可ㄎㄜˇ以ㄧˇ！」波ㄅㄛ西ㄒㄧ說ㄕㄨㄛ。

之後，他們玩了一個很吵的遊戲。

「唷呼！」波西大喊。

「咿ㄧ哈ㄏㄚ！」皮ㄆㄧ皮ㄆㄧ大ㄉㄚ叫ㄐㄧㄠ。

接著他們在花園裡度過一段美好又安靜的時光。

太ㄊㄞˋ棒ㄅㄤˋ啦ㄌㄚ！

It was a lovely day.
Pip was doing some gardening.

Posy was having fun.

"BANG! BANG!" went her drum.
"LAAA! LAAAA!" she sang.

"BOING! BOING!" she bounced.

"Could you be a bit quieter,
please, Posy?" said Pip.

Just then, Pip found a snail.
It was very friendly.

"WHEEE!"
said Posy.

"Shhhh, Posy," said Pip.

Pip gave the snail some lettuce to eat.
The snail looked happy.

Posy appeared.
"BRRM! BRRM! BRRM!" she shouted.

The snail disappeared inside its shell.

"Posy!" said Pip.
"You've scared my
snail! Your games are
too noisy! Go away!"

Posy felt sad.
She hadn't meant to scare the snail.

Poor Posy!

Pip raked
the earth.

He planted
some seeds.

And he sprinkled the seeds
with his watering can.

Pip didn't notice a bird looking at the snail.

The bird got closer. And closer.

And closer!

Oh dear!

"RRRRRRAAAAAAA!" roared a voice.
Pip jumped.

"GO AWAY, YOU BIG, GREEDY BIRD!"
shouted the voice again.

The bird flew
into the sky . . .

and the snail
dropped to the
ground.

Posy came out from behind the bush.

"Oh, Posy,"
said Pip.
"It was YOU!
Your loud voice
saved the snail!"

"I'm sorry, Posy," said Pip.
"Sometimes it's really good to be noisy.

Can we be friends again?"

"Yes, of course we can!" said Posy.

After that, they played a very NOISY game.

"WHOO-HOO!" shouted Posy.

"YEE-HAA!" shouted Pip.

And then they had a nice quiet time in the garden.

Hooray!

作者簡介

繪者簡介

譯者簡介

卡蜜拉‧里德　Camilla Reid

卡蜜拉‧里德在出版界資歷超過20年，長期致力於為小讀者們創造優質圖書。自從生了兩位小寶貝以後，她也逐漸在奇特且迷人的幼兒領域培養起敏銳洞察力，陸續創作了許多暢銷的繪本、操作書和圖文書。

阿克賽爾‧薛弗勒　Axel Scheffler

1957年出生於德國漢堡市，25歲時前往英國就讀巴斯藝術學院。他的插畫風格幽默又不失優雅，最著名的當屬《古飛樂》（Gruffalo）系列作品，不僅榮獲英國多項繪本大獎，譯作超過40種語言，還曾改編為動畫，深受全球觀眾喜愛，是世界知名的繪本作家。薛弗勒現居英國，持續創作中。

酪梨壽司

當過記者、玩過行銷，在紐約和東京流浪多年後，終於返鄉定居的臺灣媽媽。出沒於臉書專頁「酪梨壽司」與個人部落格「酪梨壽司的日記」。